To Franz, Juno, Quillow, Ebenezer, Pignolia, Smee, Winnie,
Pogo, Pippa, and Bunky, and to Bob, who is a person
LS

Thank you to Amy Berniker and all the wonderful people
at Candlewick! And a special thanks to Chris Paul
PM

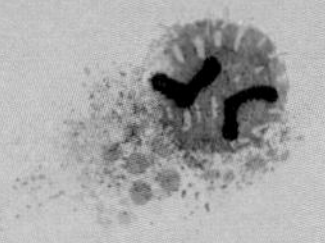

First edition 2021

Library of Congress Catalog Card Number pending
ISBN 978-1-5362-0309-7

21 22 23 24 25 26 CCP 10 9 8 7 6 5 4 3 2 1

Printed in Shenzhen, Guangdong, China

This book was typeset in Badger.
The illustrations were done in pen and ink, watercolor, and acrylic
on Strathmore paper and digitally enhanced.

Candlewick Press
99 Dover Street
Somerville, Massachusetts 02144

www.candlewick.com

DOGS LOVE CARS

LEDA SCHUBERT illustrated by PAUL MEISEL

CANDLEWICK PRESS

Dogs love cars.

Any car, old or new.
Windows down, noses out, ears flapping,
smelling grass and trees, smelling people,
smelling other dogs.
Drooling on the glass—
car wash!

Dogs love walks.

Short walks and long walks,
up hills and down,
walks in cities and countryside,
fast and slow walks,
off leash and on.
Oops!

Dogs love dogs.

Big dogs, little dogs,
dachshunds and goldendoodles,
barking, licking, smelling,
wagging, chasing, running,
falling down, rolling, getting up.
Bathtime!

Dogs love napping.

Outside, inside, in the car,
on rugs, couches, chairs,
on your feet, on your lap,
on dog beds and no bed.
And anywhere.

BUGS!

Dogs love toys.

New toys and old toys,
stuffed toys and chewies,
squeaky toys and quiet toys,
hard toys and soft toys.
People toys!

Uh-oh!

Dogs love chores.

Stacking and unstacking wood,
fetching balls and sticks,
burying and unburying bones,
bringing the paper and the mail,
washing and unwashing cars.
Come here, puppy!

Dogs love school.

Sitting, staying,
lying down.
Coming when called.
Lots of “good dog!” treats.
Learning—
and forgetting!

Dogs love people.

Old people, young people,
tall people, small people,
and tiny babies.
Sometimes too much!

Dogs love food.

Most food.
Dog food, tasty treats,
biscuits and butter,
chicken and cheese,
other dogs' food,
your food.
Watch out!

Dogs love cats.

Sometimes.

But most of all,

DOGS LOVE YOU,

all the time.